Racoo Racoo
The Magical Shoes

Rachel Ruth

Ilustrations by Hank Lamlech

Rachel Ruth

Once upon a time, there were two sisters. Neither one was more wonderful than the other, while Kayla was flawed with feet that were too large, her older sister Lily had a jealous heart.

Kayla, being naïve, was always trusting of Lily's good judgment, but unbeknownst to her Lily was hatching a wicked plot. Lily got a pair of wonderful shiny black shoes for the Spring Musical, as Kayla still searched far and wide to no avail.

Alas, they arrived at Paylitte, where they found but only one pair of shoes to fit Kayla's feet. Kayla was unsure she liked them, because they were pink patent alligator flats with ankle straps.

Now, jealous Lily seized the opportunity to look better than her sister and reassured Kayla that she would have the most beautiful shoes at the musical. Upon their arrival at home, Lily bolted from the car and screamed:

"Racoo Racoo
Those are the ugliest shoes.
They're alligator pink,
they're huge and they stink,
and don't you think
I'll always be prettier than you?"

Then Kayla ran into the house and cried, "Mommy, mommy, my feet are too big."

"My darling girl, those are the feet that you were born with and will die with. You are a beautiful girl, and it doesn't matter what size feet you have," consoled her mother.

Still upset, Kayla fled to her room, where she put her new shoes back in their box, and then flung herself upon the bed and cried, "Why did I ever listen to my sister Lily? I should never have picked those dreadful shoes. They make my feet look like bobsleds."

All at once, from the corner of her room she heard a muffled cry. Startled, she bolted upright on her bed.

"Who's there?" she queried.

"Take us out, take us out," a soft voice replied.
Cautiously Kayla inched her way to the corner of her bed and peered over.
Again, she asked, "Who's there?"
"We're down here. Take us out," the voice replied.
Kayla reached down and picked up the shoe box, and placed
it on her bed.

"Racoo, Racoo
We're magical shoes
Slip us on
and the most beautiful one
will be you."

Opening the box, she slipped on the shoes. Then suddenly, in a blinding
flash of pink patent light, she was transformed into the most beautiful
maiden in all the city.

Lily, curious to see the torment she had caused her little sister, had been watching through a crack in Kayla's door. Observing the magical

transformation, she said to herself, "I must have those shoes. No one can be more beautiful than I at the musical."

Then Lily retreated to her room and began to plan the scheme to the get the shoes.

Frightened of the transformation the shoes had caused, Kayla slipped them off and hid them under her bed. As she pulled down the bedspread, she heard a knock at the door. It was Lily.

"Can I come in? I'd like to talk to you."

"Why should I let you in? You made fun of my shoes," Kayla cried.

"Oh, I'm so sorry dear sister, and I lied about your shoes. I think they're beautiful, but if you feel unsure about wearing them to the musical, then you can wear my new shiny black shoes."

Unsure of what to do, Kayla, once again trusted her big sister and relinquished the pink patent alligator flats with ankle straps to Lily, who with glee handed Kayla her shiny black shoes.

The day of the musical arrived at last, and Kayla—busy— preparing herself chose her pink chiffon dress which fit perfectly, unlike her sister's shiny black shoes that were way too small. She had to feverishly work at squeezing her feet and curling toes like cheese curls to make them fit into the front of the shoes as her heels hung out the backside.

Meanwhile, Lily was busy stuffing paper in the toes of the pink patent alligator flats with ankle straps, so they would fit her feet. Then searching her closet high and low for something to wear that would match the shoes, she only found a red and yellow tartan plaid dress.

Then their mother called from downstairs, "Come along, come along, girls, or we'll be late."

The girls rushed down the stairs and their mother gasped.

"Lily, whatever are you doing with your sister's shoes on, and why did you pick that dress?"

Lily turned and snarled like an idol named Billy and laughed.

"Don't worry, Mother, with these shoes I'll be the most beautiful maiden at the musical."

Not having time to argue, their mother rushed the sisters off. As they entered the auditorium, Kayla gracefully limped to her seat, as Lily fought to keep the magical shoes on her feet as her heels slipped out with each step she took. One by one the entire audience began to notice the silly girl in the tartan plaid dress with the humongous shoes that were making a calamity of clapping noises as she walked down the aisle.

"Look at her," someone said.

"Check out those pink shoes," said another.

"Have you ever seen anything so crazy?" exclaimed one more as Lily approached her chair.

As she started to turn and sit down, a snicker arose as she stepped entirely out of the left shoe. Then the snicker mushroomed into peels of laughter. In total humiliation, Lily hurled the shoes at Kayla and sprinted out of the auditorium.

During the musical, Kayla heard:

> "Racoo Racoo
> Your dreams will come true.
> We're magical shoes
> because we fit you."

She reached under her chair and put on her magical pink patent alligator flats with ankle straps. Then all at once, a blinding pink patent flash filled the auditorium. The audience was in awe and never before had so many people witnessed such a bright light. As the musical ended and the people started to file out, Kayla rose and caught everyone's eye.

Exclamations were heard all over the auditorium.

"Look, she's the most beautiful maiden at the musical."

"Those pink patent alligator flats with ankle straps and pink chiffon dress are perfect for her."

As Kayla reached the exit door, the most handsome boy reached out and touched her. He said, "Those are some awesome pink patent alligator flats with ankle straps. Do you want a lemonade?"

Being the timid soul that she was, Kayla asked, "Who are you?"

He replied, "My name is Tim, and my dad owns this auditorium. You can have as many lemonades and candy bars as you want if you hang out with me."

Unworldly but not stupid, Kayla couldn't turn down the beautiful sparkly ring… or his offer of candy bars and lemonade.

Lily was distraught by her sister's good fortune and spent the rest of her life searching all the Paylittle stores throughout the city for a pair of pink patent alligator flats with ankle straps to fit her feet.

The moral to this story is:
Racoo, Racoo
Take the feet that you grew.
Have pride in yourself
and good things will come true.

THE END

In the blinding light of
a pink patent flash,
every girl should remember
her favorite shoes of the past.
RACOO RACOO
The magic of new shoes
is in the feet that you grew,
so wear them with pride
and be the beautiful you.

A special thanks to Naomi Wargel, Anita Williams, Nick Williams - Conceptual Imput
Hank Lamlech - Illustrations, Fawn Martz - Graphic Design,
Theresa Lacey – CopyEditing, Michael Ilacqua – Cover design
and John O'Melveny Woods, my Publisher.